The All-American Jump and Jive Jig

written by M.P. Hueston ✳ illustrations by Amanda Haley

STERLING

New York / London

All across the country, there are dances children do.
Different kinds in different towns, and you can learn them, too!

Come along and we'll be off, as we begin our quest
To find fun moves in far-off places North, South, East, and West.

Up in Maine is where we will discover our first bop.
Sam and Shane will show us how to do the Rockland Sock-Hop.

Take your shoes off, don't be shy. Put on your favorite socks.
Hop up and down and all around, watch out for toys and blocks!

Another neat New England groove, which comes from Massachusetts,
Is called the Boston Tea Party, and Katie loves to do it.

Shimmy like a boiling kettle,
whistle for some tea.

Make a spout and tip it down
to pour a cup for me.

In New York City playgrounds, Ian, Eddie, and their friends
Do the **Brooklyn Boogie** until their playdates end.
The Brooklyn Boogie's easy, and they'll teach it to us now.

Your arms go up,

You stomp around,

and then
you **take** a bow.

Down the coast a little ways, in Mid-Atlantic states,
Kids enjoy the D.C. Freeze—and Keisha thinks it's great.

While the music's playing **dance** as silly as you choose.

When you hear the music stop, **stand** still like a statue.

Patriot

A cool new dance in Florida has got a Latin beat.
Miami Mambo is its name, it'll make you move your feet.

Swing your hips from side to side; Sofia has the knack.
Slide your right foot forward while you step your left foot back.

Girls and boys down South agree that their dance is just grand.
William and Ella lead the parade as we try the Dixieland Band.
Pick an instrument you'd like to play: trombone, triangle, trumpet.

Now march around

and make some noise,

grab a big bass drum

and thump it.

There are lots of funny dances that kids do near the Great Lakes.
One Michigan invention is the Mackinac Milk Shake.

Jake and Jordan know the moves, let's practice till we've got 'em.
Shake your head and shake your hands, your belly, back, and bottom.

Across our nation's fruited Plains the children jump and jiggle.
That's why the dance they like best is called the Midwest Wiggle.

Hailey and Ben are about to start. Let's join them, are you ready?
Flap your arms and twist your hips and bend your legs like spaghetti.

Up and down the Lone Star State all little guys and gals
Do the Lubbock Line Dance just like Buddy and his pals.

Stand in a row

kick your feet up in the air.

and link your arms,

If no brothers, sisters, or friends are home, line up your teddy bears.

Another fun Southwestern strut is quite simple to explain.
Daniel knows the steps by heart, it's the **Albuquerque Airplane**.

Spread your arms like two strong wings, start your engines: Zoom! Zoom!
Tilt to the **left** and to the **right** and **fly** around the room.

Kids all along the Rockies, from Boulder up to Butte,
Do the Elevation Celebration, Claire and Carlos look so cute!

Use your arms and legs to climb the mountain's sloping side,
Shade your eyes when you reach the top to gaze out far and wide.

Our next stop is Oregon, for Grace and Maggie's trick.
What's all the rage in their hometown is the Portland Pogo Stick.

Pretend you're on this springy pole, hold tight to the handlebars.
Now bounce and boing and bounce again, you just might touch the stars!

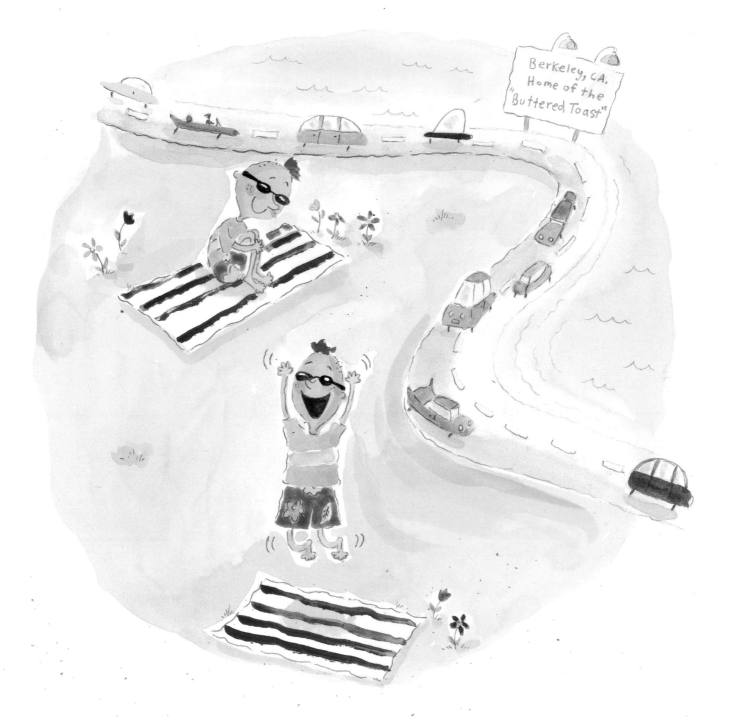

The road is very scenic heading south along the coast.
On California's sunny shores we'll learn the Berkeley Buttered Toast.

Zachary will show us how to **crouch low** to the ground.
Then **pop up** from a toaster and spread butter **up** and **down**.

Far out on the Pacific, where Hawaii's palm trees sway,
Children do the **Hilo Hula**, Pearl and Maya lead the way.

Gently **strum** a ukulele,
play a pretty island tune.

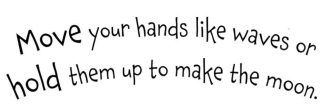

Move your hands like waves or
hold them up to make the moon.

Atop Alaska's frosty peaks every boy and girl
knows the Juneau Jitterbug. Let's all give it a whirl!

Imagine you're an insect, like a cricket or a flea.
Now flit and flutter, creep and crawl. James buzzes like a bee.

So gather friends from everywhere who want to have some fun
To make a brand-new dance by mixing all steps into one.

The All-American Jump

Stomp, shake, wiggle, hop!

Is how it could start out.

Kick, fly, bounce, pop! and Jive Jig!

Now let's all give a shout.

(Hurray!)

But what to call this innovation? It should be something big.
I know—How about **The All-American Jump and Jive Jig!?**

Let's all **jump** and **jive** and **jig** till the sun sets in the West.
And when at last we finish—well, it's time to take a rest.

Thanks for coming with us, now our busy day is done.
What dances do you like to do with your friends where you're from?